Surrender

Angela Ford

Surrender

Thank you to all those at Books to Go Now who made this book possible with the best cover!

And a special thank you to my editor (MM).

Endless thanks to my children (Devon & Shaylyn) & my very patient man (Tim) for their support and understanding of all the hours I spend writing.

Look for Angela Ford's Other titles with Books to Go Now

Closure

Unforgettable Kiss

Forbidden

Blind Tasting

The Christmas Wreath

The Love List

Christmas Forever

Copyright © 2015 Angela Ford

All rights reserved.

ISBN-13:978-1507565018

ISBN-10:1507565011

Excerpt from Surrender

"You need to relax. Don't take this the wrong way, but you're very uptight," Brett informed her.

"I have every right to be uptight. My husband just died. Someone wants me dead. You're parading around naked. I'm stuck in a dingy motel room—with no air conditioning I might add."

"There's only one way to shut you up." Brett smiled and took her in his arms quickly and kissed her.

Lauren took a step back and looked at him. She wasn't sure whether to slap him or kiss him. An inevitable desire to kiss him answered for her. Her hands touched his chest. She felt his heart pound. He hadn't yet dressed. She felt his arousal against her. His lips parted. His fresh-showered scent drove her senses wild. Nothing else mattered at this moment. Desire overcame her as she met his inviting kiss. His lips brushed against hers, as the thought of danger left her thoughts. The fact she'd just buried her husband no longer registered. She opened her mouth to deepen his kiss and the outside world disappeared. She stepped back toward the bed. He followed her lead without letting go of the kiss. A tangled mess led to tangled sheets as they devoured every inch of each other's bodies.

Justice that love gives is a surrender, justice that law gives is a punishment. –Gandhi

Chapter One

"Stay here!" Narcotics Agent Brett Donovan ordered and reached for his gun. He pointed it away from her and released the safety.

Lauren Reynolds froze. Startled fear raced through her veins. Agent Donovan said they would come back to finish the job.

Agent Donovan turned off the light and opened the door slightly and looked through the crack down the darkened hallway. He swiftly placed his back against the wall and held his gun in an upright position. "Lock the door and call 911," he told her.

His calm voice settled her enough to follow his order. She locked the bedroom door and picked up her phone. With trembling fingers, she dialed 911.

"There's someone in my house planning to kill me," Lauren frantically whispered. The 911 operator asked for her name, address and if she was alone. She told the operator about Agent Donovan then took a quick breath and felt relieved when the operator told her help was on the way. The sudden sound of a gunshot made her jump. Lauren dropped her phone and sucked in a quick breath. She stepped back and hid behind the tall chest of drawers. She shook in fear in the dark. She didn't move. She couldn't. *Why is this happening to me?*

Still dressed in her black Chanel suit, Lauren nervously played with the classic string of pearls that hung around her neck. Her matching hat still lay on the bed. All she removed after the funeral were the black heels she'd just bought at Saks Fifth Avenue the day before. Appearance always remained of the upmost importance to Lauren Reynolds. She loved her husband and mourned his death. Then Agent Donovan knocked on her door with the shocking news that her husband's death was not an accident.

Lauren Reynolds came from money, the only child of the Vanderholms of New Jersey, born with a silver spoon in her mouth. Her parents wanted her to marry someone from their world but Lauren chose John Reynolds. He owned an import/export business in Jersey. A well-known and respected businessman, John did not come from old money. His warehouse shipped domestic goods around the world—or so Lauren believed. She fell deeply in love with John. She became a widow before their first anniversary.

An explosion in John's warehouse took his life. The police closed the case as an accident. Lauren's family and closest friends gathered after the funeral. She assumed the knock at her door would be a friend who'd forgotten something. Lauren opened the door to a sexy rugged-looking man who flashed a badge.

"FBI Narcotics Agent Brett Donovan, I'd like to talk to you about your husband's murder." He stressed her husband's death was not an accident and her life was in danger.

She let him in.

"Thank you Mrs. Reynolds. I'm sorry to drop by on the day of the funeral, but word on the street is there's a hit out for you." Agent Donovan told her that her husband had been involved with the drug cartel and shipped drugs from his warehouse.

Lauren didn't want to believe him.

"That is absurd! Please leave." Lauren stormed up her spiral staircase from the front foyer.

Agent Donovan followed her into her bedroom. She tossed her hat on the bed and threw her shoes into the closet.

"I didn't mean to upset you Mrs. Reynolds, especially today." He spoke with compassion.

"Then why did you come? The police told me the explosion was an accident. How dare you suggest my husband was involved with the drug cartel?" Lauren shouted. Before she could say another word, she heard a noise downstairs.

"Is there anyone in the house with you?" he asked and quietly shut the bedroom door.

"No, everybody left," she replied, startled.

When the doorknob rattled a few moments later, Lauren peered around the edge of the chest of drawers. She hadn't moved.

"Mrs. Reynolds, its Agent Donovan."

The sound of his voice relieved her enough to slowly walk toward the door and unlock it.

"It's safe to come out now." He spoke calmly.

She wondered how he could be so calm as she shook uncontrollably.

"Perhaps a drink will calm your nerves." He suggested to her.

"Great idea, I could use a double." Lauren walked out of the bedroom and motioned for him to follow. She led him downstairs and into her husband's cigar room.

"Would you like me to mix the drinks?" He offered. She watched him eye the selection of her husband's cigars after mixing the drinks.

"Help yourself. Take them all if you'd like. I never did like the smell when John…" She paused and a tear formed in her eye. For a moment she wished she could smell the scent. At least then John would be alive.

Agent Donovan politely declined, "No thank you, I don't smoke. I know it's a lot to digest Mrs. Reynolds." Brett handed her a drink.

"Thank you," she said and took the drink.

Agent Donovan's phone rang. "I'm sorry, it's my superior. I have to take this."

Lauren listened to the agent's side of the conversation. He mentioned to his superior that he'd arrived at the Reynolds home. She heard him reiterate the attempt on her life and he'd fired a shot but the man got away. He pressed the end button on his phone and turned to face Lauren when the doorbell rang. Lauren attempted to leave the room but he stopped her.

"It's not safe. Allow me to answer the door." He strongly suggested she remain in the cigar room.

Lauren stood at the entrance to the cigar room. From there she saw him open the door to two police officers and could hear their conversation.

"Agent Brett Donovan, FBI." He extended his hand to each officer.

"Officer O'Brien and this is Officer Taylor. The 911 operator mentioned an agent onsite. She also mentioned an intruder. Is this correct?"

Agent Donovan nodded. "Yes, that is correct. Please come in." He motioned the officers toward Lauren and introduced her.

"This is Lauren Reynolds and this is her home. I came for her husband's funeral today. Family and friends just left when we heard a noise. I fired my gun when I saw a dark shadow in the kitchen but did not hit him. Once the intruder realized he wasn't alone, he fled through the back door."

Lauren couldn't believe what she heard. *Why the hell is he not telling them about the assigned hit and my husband's murder?*

"Is this correct Mrs. Reynold's?" Officer O'Brien asked. Lauren looked at Agent Donovan who slightly shook his head. She figured he didn't want her to mention anything about the hit out for her. Brett made it sound like a simple break-and-enter. Confused she nodded. "Yes Officer."

The officers then asked if they could check the kitchen and the remainder of the house. Agent Donovan offered to show them around.

"Let me take you. It's been a long emotional day for Mrs. Reynolds. She needs to rest."

He led Lauren to the sofa and handed her drink to her. Questions raced through her mind. She decided to wait until the officers left before she drilled the agent. She lifted the glass to her lips. The alcohol soothed her anxiety. The officers came back to the cigar room and reminded her to alarm the house after they left. She nodded in agreement. Agent Donovan informed the officers he would take her to her family's home and walked them to the door.

"Why did you tell them it was a possible robbery? Why didn't you tell them what you told me?" Lauren finally spoke sharply at him.

"Our investigation has been undercover for the past year. The local police have no clue about your husband's business. For now we are going to keep it that way," he told her in a warning tone.

"For now" She stormed across the room, inches away from him. She stood eye-to-eye with Agent Donovan at five-foot-ten.

He didn't move and didn't say a word.

"Some man just tried to kill me. You're the one who just told me there's a hit out for me. Why the hell didn't you tell the officers that?" Anger raced through her veins. Her dad always told her she's as fiery as her red hair.

"I'm not blowing the investigation. Not now. I'm too close to crack it wide open," Agent Donovan answered in a sharp tone of voice. Lauren looked deeply into his eyes for some sort of compassion. She heard compassion in his voice earlier, but now he seemed cold. His eyes were the one thing that did catch her attention. They were piercing green. His dark long eyelashes only enhanced the color. His messed hair and five o'clock shadow gave him such a sexy look. The scent of his cologne teased her senses. Lauren shook her head loose of those thoughts and remembered her anger with him. More so, she'd buried her husband just hours before. She sighed heavily. She noticed his eyes drop to her chest as she took a deep breath. He smiled. This angered her more and she spun around and walked to the phone by the bar. He followed her and grabbed the phone from her hand.

"No phone calls," he said harshly.

"You don't own me. Give me the damn phone. I'm calling my father."

"Your father can't protect you. Neither can the police. But I can."

Lauren took another deep breath and rolled her eyes. *Who the hell does he think he is? Does he know who my father is?* Her eyes widened. She wondered if he read minds.

"Your father's money can't protect you. The people that want you dead don't care about your money. They just want to finish the job."

"Why? I don't know anything about my husband's business. I was never a part of it. I'm not even sure I believe you. John was a good man. He wouldn't get involved with people like that." She stormed past him and went upstairs.

"Do I have to chase you around this house all night just to talk to you?" He hollered out to her.

She stopped and turned. "You can always leave." She threw the words at him and continued up the stairs.

He found her seated at the end of her bed. He leaned against the doorway with his arms folded. She looked up at him. Her mind raced about the tall sexy, rugged-man that stood at her doorway. Her thoughts shocked her. Her husband just died and she was supposed to be grieving not desiring another man. She shrugged it off in the belief she was just confused. She'd been grieving and then he showed up and threw this information in her face. Then with someone in the house and the sound of a gunshot; she felt sure confusion, exhaustion and anger took over.

"I won't leave. I'm here to protect you. Trust me. I will."

Lauren wasn't sure if his ego just spoke or if he actually cared. The man rattled her.

"Fine, I'm too tired to argue with you. I'm going to bed. Please close my door." She got up from the bed, walked into her bathroom and shut the door. Part of her felt relieved he would protect her.

Chapter Two

Brett found his way to the kitchen. *It's going to be a long night*, he thought. He started a pot of coffee and went to his car to grab his briefcase. He decided to work even though there were several bedrooms in the mansion to grab a bed for the night. Exhausted from the drive from Washington which preceded the redeye from Mexico, he could have easily taken one of those beds, but his work ethic took over. There was no time for rest and he wasn't a guest. He hadn't even been invited to the funeral, though he had known John in college. He remained on the outskirts where no one noticed him. No invitation told Brett that John hadn't mentioned his name to his new family. *Why would he?* Brett thought. The two hadn't kept in touch. After college, they went their separate ways. They both had goals to achieve.

Brett camped at the kitchen table with his coffee and files. He'd been investigating the drug cartel for three years since he joined the narcotics department at the FBI, his goal after college. He spent four years in Washington with the Secret Service until the opportunity arrived with the narcotics department: an undercover position in Mexico to bring down the drug cartel operations that filled the streets of New York. His investigations led him to John.

The discovery shocked him. John had been the most decent guy he met at college. Brett couldn't save John but he felt obligated to protect his wife. He wanted to tell Lauren, when she first opened her door, about his friendship with John in college, but he knew he couldn't let it get personal. He hadn't told his superior of his connection to John Reynolds. The case was too important to risk it. The FBI knew his parents had been at the wrong place at the wrong time when a drug deal went down. They'd been caught in the middle of a bad deal that took their lives. Brett remained cold-hearted when questioned about his parents' deaths. He led the FBI interviewer to believe he wasn't close to his parents since he chose his career path in criminology instead of his father's wish to join him in the family business. For generations, the family had been Real Estate Investors. Brett convinced the FBI he was the man for an undercover operation because he had no family and could fade into thin air without any questions to his whereabouts. His credentials for the past four years confirmed his eligibility for the job. His superior warned him not to let it get personal.

He set his coffee cup down and ran his hands through his messed hair and across his face. He'd shaved before he left Washington but the stubble had already grown back. He wasn't used to the thought of a shave and shower. For the past three years, his undercover position didn't require a clean shave. He lived in some crummy places while undercover. Before his post in Mexico, there wasn't a day that Brett Donovan wasn't dressed to perfection. His parents would have been shocked by his appearance the past few years. Then again, they were the reason he was there. He was determined to bring down the operation that took his parents' lives.

"Do you ever sleep Agent Donovan?" A sleepy soft voice startled him away from his thoughts.

He looked up from his files. Lauren stood at the kitchen doorway. Her neatly-kept soft tresses had been let loose into a wave of fiery-red curls beyond her shoulders that enhanced her hazel eyes and dark lashes. Her eyes were sharp. They took in everything in her surroundings. She was a beautiful woman any man, in his right mind would notice. He could tell she came from money. Not just by her polished appearance. She moved with confidence. Her speech and mannerisms cried out a sophisticated education. Silk wrapped her every curve and barely covered her thighs. He saw her follow his eyes down to them and back up to her chest. Her wrap, tied loosely, allowed part of her breasts to peak out from the silk that barely covered them. She smiled. He knew she saw his eyes travel, but he ignored being caught.

"Call me Brett please," he said in a tired raspy voice. He watched her move elegantly across the room.

"Already on a first-name basis, are we?" She said and helped herself to a coffee. She turned and took a sip. "You may call me Lauren."

"Can't sleep?" He tried to keep their conversation general. He wanted to change the subject and take his mind away from the thoughts that raced through it. He knew he shouldn't be thinking of her that way. She was an assignment and had been the wife of the man who had been like a brother to him in college. A man they just buried hours before.

She shook her head and then joined him at the table. "I tried to sleep." She looked around.

"John and I bought this house two weeks before our wedding. Our first night here was our wedding night and the last night he made love to me in this house. He became distant after our honeymoon in Mexico."

Brett sat quietly and listened. The sadness he seen in her eyes and her recent words made him question if it had been a loveless marriage. Then he wondered if John had confronted Nick Mendez in Mexico and told him he wanted out of their business deal.

Lauren suddenly rose from the table and began to walk out of the kitchen. She turned to him.

"I'm sorry. I didn't mean to get personal." She smiled politely.

"That's okay, Lauren. I'm a good listener."

Brett pulled out the chair beside him and motioned for her to sit. She hesitated for a moment and then joined him. He began to pick up the papers and put them back in the folder.

Lauren picked up a picture. "Who's this?"

"Nobody" He quickly grabbed the picture and placed it in the folder. She didn't question his hasty response when she noticed John's picture. He saw tears form in her eyes. Brett didn't grab the picture this time. His heart went out to her. She remained quiet as she looked at the picture of her recently-deceased husband.

"Do you recognize the man with John?" Brett quickly changed his focus back to the case.

Lauren shook her head. Her eyes hadn't left the picture.

"The man in the picture with John is Nick Mendez. He is known to run the drug cartel operation out of New York from Mexico. I've tracked him for three years. This is the man who would have assigned a hit for your husband and you," Brett told her point-blank. He didn't know how else to tell her. There wasn't time to gently break the news. He could tell his words frightened her by the look in her eyes.

"This can't be true. John is…was a decent man." She began to speak but the tears took over.

Brett reached out and covered her hand. It killed him to admit that the man who'd been like a brother to him had been caught up in this tangled mess. He hadn't accepted it in the beginning either until he dug a little deeper into John's financial records. He remembered John's determination in college. John spoke of building his own successful business. Brett knew John's brilliant mind first-hand. That's how they met. Brett needed a tutor and John saved his ass from being expelled from college. Brett's determination to stay in college and not live off his trust fund forced him to go to John. Then they became friends. John, on the other hand, didn't have that choice. He grew up in foster homes.

"I'm not saying your husband wasn't a decent man. His financial records show a fall about two years ago. The Mendez family are known to prey on opportunities like this. They probably approached your husband." Brett tried to comfort her. He imagined it to be a lot to digest at a most difficult time.

"I thought I knew my husband. I was wrong. Guess you never really know someone," Lauren sadly remarked.

The expression in her eyes grabbed his heart. He didn't know how to respond. He wanted to tell her he personally knew John had been a decent man when he knew him, but he couldn't.

"You know," Lauren said and looked into Brett's eyes. "My father didn't approve of John in the beginning. He said six months wasn't long enough to really know someone before you marry them. My father said this only because John didn't come from old money. Maybe I should have listened to him but I thought I fell in love and listened to my heart." Lauren sighed and took a deep breath.

Brett knew exactly what she meant. Her father sounded like his. He chuckled silently as he heard his father's words in his mind. *Old money does not mix well with new money. We need to remain in our own circle.*

"You were only married a few months?" Brett inquired.

"Yes. We married six months after we met. I thought I knew everything about John I needed to know," Lauren responded.

"John tried to get out of his contract with the Mendez family for that exact length of time. I believe he wanted to be a decent husband but one can't walk away from the Mendez family without consequences." Brett knew this information would not comfort her but he felt she had a right to know about John's intent. He just made the wrong choice to get involved with the drug cartel to save his business.

"That's why they killed him?" Lauren asked.

"I hoped my husband loved me more than his business. My father never did. His company always came before my mother and me."

Brett nodded. Her words saddened him. He remembered how his father's wishes mattered more than what Brett wanted.

Lauren picked up the picture again of John and that man outside John's warehouse. She turned to Brett with a horrified look.

"I remember when we were on our honeymoon in Mexico, John left me for a day. He said he had business in a nearby town. Maybe he met with this man."

Lauren waved the picture in her hand.

"Maybe that's why he became distant. I thought it might be me or the fact that he'd become so preoccupied accepting my father's partnership offer and selling the warehouse."

Lauren placed the picture on top of Brett's folder, "It doesn't matter now".

"Why me" she asked. "Why do you believe they want to kill me?"

"They're only concerned that you may know about them. That's all. To them it's just business."

Lauren seemed to swallow those words hard. She stood and walked toward the patio doors then stared into the darkened sky for a few moments. Brett sat quietly and watched her until he noticed a reflection outside. He quickly sprang up from the table. His chair knocked over as he leaped for Lauren. The bullet pierced through the glass door and just missed her. Brett had taken her down hard and covered her body with his. Silence remained in the room for a few moments before Brett spoke.

"Are you hurt?" He asked. She shook uncontrollably in silence, "No."

"Stay low and move slowly around the corner between the cabinets." Brett sat with his back against the cabinets and reached for his gun. He peeked around the corner slowly. He saw nothing but darkness beyond the patio doors. He moved suddenly toward the table and stayed behind it. There wasn't a sound and nothing but darkness outside. He reached up to flip the light switch off and hoped for a better look through the glass doors into the backyard. Still, he saw nothing. Brett moved along the back wall until he reached the patio doors. He slowly drew the blinds to cover the open glass and went to Lauren. She shook behind the cabinets with a look of terror in her eyes. He reached out for her hand. "It's safe now. Come with me."

She took his hand. "Where are we going?"

"It isn't safe to stay here. Trust me. I will keep you alive." His voice remained calm. She nodded.

****

Lauren didn't say a word and drifted to sleep in the car. When she awoke, it was still dark outside. Brett never said where they were headed. It appeared he drove toward the coast and south. For some odd reason she trusted this man she'd just met. She looked over at him. He looked exhausted.

Why is this man going out of his way to protect me? She thought.

"Are you not tired? Where are we going?" she finally asked.

"I am and where you will be safe. We'll stop soon and get some rest," he answered without taking his eyes off the road. A few miles later, he pulled into a rundown motel next to the road.

"Why are we stopping here?" Lauren asked him.

He put the car in Park and turned off the ignition, then turned to her. "I just told you we need to rest." He sounded beyond exhaustion.

"But why here?" She asked him. Lauren Reynolds had never stayed at a motel in her life. She had been used to luxury her entire life. He had been in her house. He had probably searched her financial records as well as her husband's. She figured he must know she deserved better than this.

"Sorry, it's not the Ritz, but it will have to do." He laughed.

His laugh only infuriated her more. She slammed the car door shut and stormed toward the motel entrance. *Why do I trust this man?* She wondered.

Brett locked the car. He looked around before he entered the motel. She figured he was checking to see if they'd been followed. Irritated with him, Lauren folded her arms and waited for him to check in. He took the key and thanked the frail old man who sat at the front desk.

"Follow me," Brett told her.

She felt frustrated that he had completely ignored her attitude about his decision to stay at a motel.

"Fix this air conditioner," she demanded.

He turned the switch for the air conditioner and it came off in his hand. He laughed and handed it to her. "Guess you will have to open a window."

"Do you know what the humidity factor is out there?" Lauren screamed. The past week had been unusually humid for late September. The weather called for a warmer October than usual as well.

Brett shrugged. "Hot?"

His sarcasm only ignited her temper. She stormed past him and slammed the bathroom door.

"Hot-tempered snob," Brett announced. He knocked on the door. "I'm sorry this place is a dive. I need a shower and a few hours of sleep. I promise the next place will be better."

Lauren opened the door. "And where is that Agent Donovan?" She asked.

"Ocean City"

"What the hell is in Ocean City?"

"My place"

"Bathroom is all yours." Exhausted and hot, she didn't care to argue with him anymore. She hoped his place wasn't a one-room bachelor apartment that required a torch rather than a cleaning, or she'd call her father.

Lauren looked at the motel bed and wondered if it would be clean enough to sleep on. She broke down and tears streamed down her cheeks. She wasn't sure if the tears were for John, the supposed hit or both. Beyond exhaustion, she'd cried for days and hadn't slept well. Then Agent Donovan knocked on her door and now she was stuck in a hot, dingy motel. She heard the shower stop and regained her composure. Her mother taught her to cry in private.

She felt shocked when he opened the door naked. The steam from the bathroom poured out around him and into the room. "Have you no decency?" She snapped at him. It didn't seem to bother him to be naked in front of her.

He smiled. "Forgot my bag" He walked past her.

She knew she should turn around, but she swallowed hard as she watched his bare ass when he walked across the room. He definitely kept his body toned. As quickly as that thought crossed her mind, she tried to block it. Minutes before, she'd been in tears for her husband. *Why do I keep thinking of him this way? This man infuriates me.*

"Sorry, does this bother you?" He tossed the bag on the bed and unzipped it, inches away from her. *This man definitely has a big ego.*

"No, prance around naked all night if you want. It's definitely too hot in here for clothes."

He laughed at her comment and threw the sarcasm back at her. "Feel free to do the same." Lauren gave him a smug look and he laughed louder.

"You need to relax. Don't take this the wrong way, but you're very uptight," Brett informed her.

"I have every right to be uptight. My husband just died. Someone wants me dead. You're parading around naked. I'm stuck in a dingy motel room—with no air conditioning I might add."

"There's only one way to shut you up." Brett smiled and took her in his arms quickly and kissed her.

Lauren took a step back and looked at him. She wasn't sure whether to slap him or kiss him. An inevitable desire to kiss him answered for her. Her hands touched his chest. She felt his heart pound. He hadn't yet dressed. She felt his arousal against her. His lips parted. His fresh-showered scent drove her senses wild. Nothing else mattered at this moment. Desire overcame her as she met his inviting kiss. His lips brushed against hers as the thought of danger left her thoughts. The fact she'd just buried her husband no longer registered. She opened her mouth to deepen his kiss and the outside world disappeared. She stepped back toward the bed. He followed her lead without letting go of the kiss. A tangled mess led to tangled sheets as they devoured every inch of each other's bodies.

Chapter Three

The sun's rays peaked through the ripped curtains in the motel room and Lauren opened her eyes. She felt rested for the first time in days. She remembered what happened and the smile left her face. She turned to see Brett and reality hit her hard. It *had* happened. *What was I thinking?* Guilt suddenly set in. She hadn't cheated on her husband, since he was dead, but she still felt as though she had. She snuck out of the bed quietly. She needed a shower. She thought about Brett in the shower which only added to her guilt. The man irritated her. He wasn't from her world. He'd taken her to a motel not to her liking. But then he made passionate love to her. No man had ever made her feel the way he had, not even John. She'd loved her husband and had no complaints. Brett was different. Something dark about him intrigued her. One thing she knew for certain, he definitely knew what to do in the bedroom.

"Lauren! We have to go, now!" Brett's voice and loud knock on the door startled her from her thoughts. She turned off the water and grabbed a towel. Still wet, she opened the door to find Brett with his back up against the wall by the window and gun in hand.

"What the hell is going on?" Lauren stormed across the room.

Brett grabbed her with one hand and brought her back quickly beside him. "Stay away from the window," he demanded.

His tone scared her. "Don't tell me that man tracked us here." Her lip quivered. She wondered if she was scared or cold because she stood naked and wet from the shower.

Brett must have seen the horror in her eyes. "I'm not sure. Someone knocked on the door. I looked through the peephole and saw two men. They didn't appear to be motel staff, so I ignored the knock. They've been knocking on every door. My gut tells me we need to move fast."

"Do you think they followed us to the motel?

"I feel certain someone did".

She shook as she got dressed and gathered her belongings without another word.

Brett stopped her as she reached for the door handle. "We have to go out the back."

"What back door?"

"The bathroom window" Brett grabbed their bags and led her by the hand to the bathroom.

"You want me to climb through that window?" She pointed to the small window.

"Yes and do it quickly," he snapped at her.

Without another word, she climbed through the window. Brett tossed the bags out the window first and then hoisted himself up and through. She wondered if he always lived like this. It didn't seem to bother him in the least. It appeared he embraced danger. At least he offered to carry her bag. She thought back to the night before. Both pleasure and guilt entered her mind. Those thoughts ended quickly when she heard him announce they had to walk about two miles through the woods.

"In these shoes?" she barked at him.

"You can always go back to the men who want you dead," he offered and began to walk toward the woods. Lauren grunted aloud but followed him. Anger set in and she walked quickly past him. "I wouldn't walk so fast in those, it's going to be a long walk," Brett called out to her.

She just ignored him and didn't look back. She'd reached the edge of the woods when she heard a noise from behind. She turned to see Brett swinging their bags at a man.

"Run!" Brett yelled at her.

Lauren ran between the trees and didn't look back. She could easily get around the streets of New York, but not in the woods. She hoped she ran in the right direction. It was one thing to shop all day in heels, but to run in them was another story. She ran until she couldn't and hid behind a tree. She shook in fear and tried to control her breathing. She began to pray and then wondered if it would help. Within minutes, she heard Brett's voice call out her name. She moved slowly around the edge of the tree and saw him. She ran into his embrace with great relief. He wrapped his arms around her and held her. The comfort of his arms calmed her enough to release from his hold.

"It's safe now," Brett touched her face gently and smiled.

"You keep saying that. Can this be the last time?" A tear crept down along her cheek and he wiped it away.

"I can't promise. Come on." He put his arm around her.

She still trembled. "What about that man?"

"I dealt with him, but I'm not sure where the other one is," he told her.

Lauren said no more. She felt numb. They walked silently for less than an hour before they reached the outskirts of the town. Brett's superior sent a message where they could pick up a car.

"Will I ever be able to go home?" Lauren finally spoke when Brett began to drive.

"We're close to making arrests. Until then, I will keep you alive. That I promise."

Lauren decided to accept his response. She knew she wasn't going to get more from him on the matter. She turned to look out her window. People opened their shops and began their day in the small town they drove through. She felt envious they were living their normal everyday life. She only wished she could.

"Lauren, we need to talk." Brett took her away from her moment of self-pity.

"About last night?" It was the last thing she wanted to talk about. She already carried enough guilt and decided she wanted to convince herself that it didn't happen.

"I guess we should talk about that too." He kept his eyes focused on the road.

"What do you mean? Is there something else I don't want to hear?" She quickly addressed the possibility to get out of the conversation about what happened between them. She hoped the sarcasm in her voice kept him from discussing it.

"Maybe now is not the time," Brett spoke with hesitation.

His comment only worried her. *What could he possibly tell me now? Hasn't he already turned my world upside down?* She kept quiet and hoped he'd leave it for now. She didn't desire to know any more unless he told her she could go back to her life. She knew that wasn't going to happen anytime soon and turned back to the window.

By now they had driven through the town and all she saw for miles were trees. She watched them pass by as she thought about John. A week ago he was alive and they were happy. They began to plan their first anniversary and a trip to the same resort in Mexico they did for their honeymoon. Thoughts of that only made her remember their honeymoon and how he left her one day to do business in a nearby town. It never dawned on her that his business meeting might have been with the drug cartel. She didn't know for certain but that's what now crossed her mind. *How did he get caught up in such a mess? A mess that killed him, left me running for my life, and having sex with a man I don't know?*

Chapter Four

"Sorry I'm late Marion, I had an important call." Charles Vanderholm took his seat at the head of the table and joined his wife for breakfast.

"They always are, dear," Marion replied in a sweet and respectful tone. She adored her husband. They'd been married thirty-five years and respected each other completely. Marion always thought of her marriage as more of a professional nature than one of love. It had been a pre-arranged marriage by their families. They met at her coming-out party, the debutante ball her parents had planned since she turned ten years old. They were both raised to believe old-money did not mix with new-money. They'd raised Lauren the same way, but she had a mind of her own. She laughed out loud when her mother suggested a debutante ball for her. Lauren downright refused to have such an event. She chose college instead of marriage. Her attitude infuriated her father even more when she refused to work in the family business. He almost disowned her when she brought home John Reynolds, a man who came from new-money and not from their circle. Charles did not speak to his daughter for weeks.

"I received a message late last night from Lauren," Marion told Charles when their breakfast came. Charles looked up from behind the newspaper he'd been so grossly engaged in.

"How is she?" He asked, expressionless.

Marion knew he loved his daughter despite their differences and her fiery independent ways he referred to many times over the years. Charles gave up long before to persuade her to marry into old money and become part of the family business. Charles's family had come from a long history of Investment Banking. Lauren outright told him she did not want to work in the family business because numbers bored her. He'd been upset for a long time. Being his only child, no one would continue on with the family business unless she graced him with a grandchild that might. Marion had complications with Lauren's birth and couldn't conceive again which devastated Charles. He had wanted a son to carry on the name and the business. It had always been that way. Over time he said he accepted it.

"She's grieving Charles, how do you expect her to be?"

Marion gracefully poured a coffee and sternly looked at her husband. She knew he loved his daughter and his wife but his business had always come first. A cold man who never showed any emotion; she learned over time to ignore his ways.

"She mentioned she planned to take a few days to clear her mind and not to worry."

"Good," Charles replied solemnly. Marion gave him a questioning glance.

"Don't worry Marion, she won't be gone long. If it makes you feel better, I can have her tracked," Charles addressed their daughter like a business deal.

"Best not Charles, our daughter would be furious with us. She's a grown woman. I'll wait for her to call."

Charles went back to his breakfast and reading the business section without further comment until his phone vibrated against the table.

"I assume that is an important call?" Marion asked. When he put down his paper, she took that as a yes.

"Hello? Can you please hold for a moment?" He walked over to her and kissed her on the cheek. "Have a wonderful day, my dear."

His usual routine that Marion had grown accustomed to, and about the longest time they would see each other. She'd see him in the evening for a dinner party or an event they were to attend. After that, she retired to her own bedroom before he returned home from work. It had been that way for years.

****

Charles took his call to the den and closed the door.

"Sorry I wasn't alone," he apologized for the held call and then interrupted before he could say anything else.

"There's a problem." Charles heard his caller state, sounding quite disturbed.

Charles already knew he had a problem.

"I heard the break and enter went sour. What happened?" Charles remained calm.

"An unknown man"

"Who," Charles asked.

"My man didn't recognize him."

"Then find out." Charles demanded and reminded his caller the importance of this job.

"I'm led to believe the man is one of uniform by the way my guy described his actions. Should we be worried?" The caller asked Charles.

"I don't worry. That's your department. Just get it done and quickly. I don't want this to affect my business," Charles warned the caller and ended the call. He gathered some papers from his desk and closed his briefcase. His eyes met the picture of his daughter. Charles Vanderholm quickly moved his eyes away from the picture. Business always came first.

Charles noticed Marion with her personal assistant Cheryl in the foyer on his way out. He wondered why she needed one, but she got whatever kept her happy and quiet. He did not pry. In fact he didn't really care as long as she portrayed the perfect corporate wife.

"Marion."

"Yes dear," she answered sweetly and politely excused Cheryl.

"Did Lauren mention if she had someone with her?"

"No dear, why?"

"A friend might do her some good," he lied to his wife. His only concern—his business. Everyone respected him as a well-known shrewd businessman. That's how he stayed on top. The love he showed publicly for his wife and daughter was only an act for appearance's sake. Marion wished him a good day. He waved and left without another word. She portrayed an excellent corporate wife and did her job well. He knew all Marion expected in return was a never-ending spending account.

Charles made a call once he reached his New York office. He needed to know what went wrong. There is too much at stake to risk his business or his name. He wouldn't be caught up in this mess if his daughter had listened to him in the beginning and married into old-money. She brought John Reynolds into their lives and without his blessing. Charles had done a thorough check on John and his business associates. He learned of the business association with Nick Mendez. This discovery changed Charles's mind about John. Perhaps John could be the son Charles always wanted. Then Charles began to warm up to the idea of accepting John into the family and mold him into the business. Charles set his plan in motion and pressed for an elaborate wedding. He knew Marion would convince their daughter that he would come around; at least for appearance's sake. John and Lauren were married within six months.

    Charles's plan ran smoothly. He befriended John and publicly accepted him into the family. He included John in business discussions and gatherings, the legal ones at first. Days after the wedding Charles received a call from Nick Mendez. Nick informed Charles that John had confronted Nick to end their business association because he got married and he wasn't going to screw up his dream of a family he never had. Charles calmly told Nick not to worry. After the honeymoon, Charles offered John a partnership offer he couldn't refuse. Charles believed his plan would work. After all, John had already been in business with Nick. He figured John was worried about Charles discovering the connection to Nick, but would assure him that the connection with the Mendez family was good for business. Charles convinced John he could have Lauren, the family he never had, and much more than he could ever desire.

    The plan had backfired. After the honeymoon, Charles offered John a partnership in the family business. John had been thrilled and he accepted immediately. The two had formed a bond like father and son. Charles respected John's ideas and complimented his business mind. The problem appeared when Charles held a private meeting with Nick Mendez and invited John. He only announced shock when he learned of the connection between Charles and Nick. Adamant that he wanted to run his business legally, he warned Charles he would tell Lauren, and then stormed out of the meeting. Shortly after that meeting, John went to the warehouse to meet the new owner and sign the papers. The explosion happened before the ink dried. Nobody threatened Charles Vanderholm. Nobody walked away from business with the Mendez family. Nick had taken care of the problem within an hour of John's outburst. The only concern shared between Nick and Charles if John had told his wife. Charles figured Nick wanted all loose ends tied; he knew he could not save his daughter.

John had been an orphan but Charles still checked out all foster families he had lived with. John had kept in touch with no one, not even foster parents. It appeared he had no friends in college. John had been a loner his whole life. The only connections he'd made were through his business. The few women he dated never spoke with him again. John's record came up clear. John's only connection that could ruin Charles's business was Lauren.

Charles brushed his hand over his face, frustrated to think he had missed a piece of information about John's life. His phone rang and stirred him from his thoughts.

"Do you have any news for me?" Charles got right to the point. He had waited to hear from the man who ran the search on John Reynolds months before.

"Good morning Charles. I got your message. I thought John Reynolds died. Is there a need for further investigation into his life?"

"You didn't do a thorough job. There was a man at my daughter's home last night. Find out who he is." Charles demanded.

"Yes, sir, I will get on it right away."

"Do it discretely, of course." Charles wanted an answer but he also had his reputation to uphold.

Chapter Five

Lauren hadn't said a word. Brett could respect that she didn't want to talk. He kept quiet about his connection to John and 'last night' for the time being. Now he felt hungry. They had a couple of hours before they reached Ocean City. His superior would have another car ready for him about fifty miles from his place. Used to being undercover, Brett knew the importance of shaking anyone from his tail. He pulled the car into a diner off the road. Lauren tossed him an empty look.

"I know, it's still not the Ritz, but I'm hungry. We must eat." Brett felt empathy for her. He knew how she lived and tried to understand how difficult this must all be for her.

"I'm not hungry," she announced rather stubbornly.

"I am and you can't stay here alone." Brett opened the door for her and she pouted as she followed him into the run-down diner. He pointed to a back-corner booth to keep their visibility low, and then followed Lauren, observing everyone in the diner as they passed by. He felt safe enough to quickly grab a bite to eat. He ordered for both of them. He hoped she might eat something. Lauren picked at her food. Brett inhaled his.

"Are you done?" he asked. She'd barely touched it.

"I told you I wasn't hungry," she snapped back.

Brett ignored her tone, stood up and left money on the table. "It's time to go."

Lauren got into the car and removed her shoes immediately. She rubbed her feet.

"Sore?" he asked with genuine concern.

"You try running in these shoes through the woods, and then walk for miles afterward!"

Brett keyed the ignition and began to drive. He knew he couldn't say anything to make her feel better. He remained focused on his assignment to keep her alive. He ignored what his heart felt. The flashbacks of her in his arms, his lips against hers, made it difficult.

They stopped not long after the diner. Brett pulled into a parking lot behind a second-hand store. He knew another snobbish comment would come his way.

"First a dive-motel, then a run-down diner; now a second-hand store." Lauren threw a fiery-eyed look at Brett. "Have you no clue that I am a Vanderholm?"

Brett smiled only to irritate her further.

"I refuse to go in there!"

He held the car door open and waited for her to storm past him again. It started to become a usual routine and a rather amusing one to him.

"My job is to keep you alive. Your job is to follow my orders."

He motioned for her to get out of the car. Her eyes were on fire as she exhaled a quick breath. Lauren entered the second-hand store standing out like a sore thumb. Not just by the way she dressed in a Chanel pant suit, but with her snobbish attitude. She stood with her arms crossed and a pout on her face while Brett picked out a new outfit for her disguise.

"These should fit." He handed her a pair of jeans and a T-shirt. He figured he knew her size. His hands had travelled every curve of her body the night before. Making love to her burned in his memory. He shook those thoughts and remained focused. Brett had one-night stands before. This one was different. He wondered why. He couldn't get her out of his thoughts and it wasn't the assignment to protect her. Lauren grabbed the clothes from his hand after he ordered her into the changing room and to bring the clothes she'd been wearing. He went to pay for the items.

"What are those for?" Lauren tossed her clothes at him and Brett placed them in a bag. He did not want her to stand out the way she did. He knew she wasn't happy with him but at least now she would blend in. The clothes she'd worn were fine for shopping at Saks, but not on the run.

"They are for your feet. They'll be more comfortable than the things you're wearing now," Brett smirked.

"I don't do flip-flops," she informed him.

"You do now." Brett held open the bag he had her old clothes in.

Lauren threw her heels in the bag and put on the flip-flops and stormed out the door. Brett followed with a smile. He actually enjoyed her temper tantrums.

"Where are we off to now Agent?"

The tone in Lauren's voice only made him chuckle. Brett pulled into the parking lot of a small coffee shop. He parked and smiled at Lauren. "We will meet my superior here to change cars. I need to get you to Ocean City without being followed. I will keep you alive." He grabbed their bags from the trunk and walked around to her door.

"Kevin Williams…Lauren Reynolds." Brett introduced them then tossed their bags in Kevin's car.

Kevin held out his hand, "It's nice to meet you Mrs. Reynolds. I only wish it were under better circumstances."

Lauren simply nodded and smiled politely. Brett opened the car door for her. She remained quiet.

"She hasn't said too much lately." Brett informed Kevin after he closed her door.

"Do you blame her?" Kevin asked.

Brett spoke with Kevin for a few minutes and joined Lauren in the car. The drive to Ocean City remained a quiet one. Brett understood she'd been through a lot and didn't push for a conversation. He figured she'd talk when ready.

Lauren gasped. "This is your home?" as Brett pulled into the driveway of an extravagant beach home.

"I told you it would be better than the dingy motel. I hope you will be more comfortable here." Brett smiled. He could tell by the expression on her face that she was pleased.

"I expected a one-room dirty bachelor apartment that might require a torch," she blurted out.

Brett laughed. "That would be my place in Mexico."

Lauren got out of the car and watched Brett open the first of three garage doors and parked the car inside. He closed the door and met Lauren in the driveway. She hadn't moved. She appeared mesmerized with his home.

"This is magnificent." She smiled at him.

"It's good to see you smile, Lauren. I know the past twenty-four hours have been hard on you." Brett put his arm around her without thinking and then eased back.

"Come on, I'll give you the grand tour."

"Remarkable," Lauren announced as she entered the front foyer.

"How the hell do you afford this on a cop's salary?"

The elaborate exterior of cedar and redwood made the three-story home stand out. But the exquisite interior design was something one would only see in a magazine. She watched Brett disarm the house at a keyboard mounted on the wall in the front foyer. At the touch of buttons, the window shades began to rise. Windows spanned the entire back of the house and with the cathedral ceilings, the sunlight penetrated deep throughout the house.

Brett smiled. "I changed my name when I was in college. It used to be Brett Donnelly."

Lauren flashed him a questioning look, "As in the New York real estate Donnelley?"

"That's my father and grandfather, not me. I never wanted to go into the family business. My father never forgave me for not following in his footsteps and changing my name," Brett remarked sadly.

"You wanted to be a cop?"

"Since I was a young boy, actually I always wanted to work with the FBI," Brett shared.

It was unlike him. He never shared with anyone, except John Reynolds in college. It surprised him he'd shared personal information with Lauren. He wondered if he truly had feelings for her.

"How did you end up in Mexico?"

"That's a long story. I don't want to bore you. Would you like that grand tour now?"

He quickly changed the subject. He may have shared a piece of personal information but to get into the reason why he ended up in Mexico wasn't something he shared with anyone. Not John. Not his superior.

She respected his privacy and asked no further questions. She smiled, "Great idea."

He positioned his arm for her to loop hers through for the tour. Lauren looked up at Brett.

"You know you're not the only great listener."

He smiled and nodded. He began describing the house to her but what she'd said touched his heart. There hadn't been anyone in his life that cared since his parents and only serious relationship died. His father may have been pissed that he didn't join the family business and that he changed his name to join the Secret Service, but Brett had been loved by his parents. He just never confided that to anyone.

****

Impressed with Brett's home she noted he definitely had exquisite taste in furnishings. She wondered if he had done any of it himself or hired someone. There were many family heirlooms throughout the house that Brett thoroughly described to her. *He comes from old money. My father would be impressed.* She wondered why she thought that. It wasn't like they were dating. She was Brett's assignment but she wasn't an assignment the night before. Then Lauren began to wonder if it had been part of the assignment to calm her and keep her quiet, or if he actually wanted to make love to her. She wondered why she even thought of her father and whether he approved. It wasn't as though she ever cared what he thought. Lauren loved her father but she was closer to her mother. Her mother always told her not to argue with her father and he would come around, if not for caring but for appearance sake. Lauren had been taught that at a young age. It was true. Her father had lightened and accepted John into the family. Though it did surprise her even though her mother assured her it had been for appearance sake. Lauren found it odd for her father to not only accept John into the family, but make him a partner in his business. She'd shrugged these thoughts aside because of her love for John and she wanted to be happy. Lauren had convinced herself that her father found the son he always wanted to continue the family business, and left it at that.

The second floor consisted of a luxurious master suite with a fireplace and a hot tub on the balcony.

"The best spot to watch the most spectacular sunsets," Brett said and pointed to the hot tub.

He tossed his bag on the four-poster king sized bed and motioned her into the hallway to continue the tour.

She wondered if the hot tub was an invitation for later. Her mind kept travelling off course but she smiled without comment as she shook off her thoughts and reminded herself that she'd just buried her husband the day before. Lauren noticed the photo on his bedside table. She picked up the framed picture and turned to Brett.

"This is the same picture you had on my kitchen table last night."

But Brett ignored her and walked out of the room. She followed him and grabbed his arm, "Brett, are these people your parents?"

He turned to her with sadness in his eyes. "Yes."

"Are they caught up in this mess too?"

"No, they're not. They're dead." Brett's quick direct tone told her he didn't want to talk about them. His eyes told her something different.

"What happened to them?" Lauren reached out and touched his arm gently.

"They were in the wrong place at the wrong time. They were senseless murders."

Brett shrugged his shoulders and continued down the hall describing the other three rooms on the second floor; a den and two guest bedrooms, neither of which looked like they'd ever been used. The den definitely looked more lived in than any other room in the house. This didn't surprise Lauren. From the short time she'd known Brett, it seemed like work consumed his life. He'd placed her bag on the bed in the room beside his. She wondered if he was being a gentleman or if he thought the night before had been a mistake. The third floor had a library, theatre room and a gym. Lauren followed, listening to him, and didn't ask any more about his parents. She sensed his pain and thought it best to change the subject.

"You have a spectacular home Brett." Thank you for the tour.

"I promised you it would be better than that dingy motel," he said and smiled.

And for some reason I think I would rather be in that dingy motel room again with you, no air, a steam-filled room and your naked body, she thought.

"Hungry?" His question startled her out of her desirable image of him.

"Is food always on your mind?"

"Yes." He laughed.

"Actually, I am hungry."

"It's been three years since I've been in my kitchen. I've missed it."

"You've been in Mexico for three years?" Lauren followed him down the stairs, surprised and shocked he'd been away from his beautiful home for so long.

"As I told you before, it's a long story." Brett continued down the stairs without a glance back at her.

"I have the time since you won't let me get back to my own life." Lauren laughed. She almost believed for a moment she'd become accustomed to being on the run. He pulled out a stool at the island in the middle of the kitchen for her to have a seat.

"Its top secret and I would have to kill you after I told you." He laughed.

She figured he was joking, she hoped anyway. *He wouldn't be the only one wanting to kill her these days.*

"Agent Donovan, you continue to surprise me. You have all of this but choose Mexico and the drug cartel instead, and it appears you are a master chef in the kitchen."

Brett looked over his shoulder and smiled. "I love to cook and I'm always hungry."

"So Agent, what other secrets do you have?"

Brett grabbed a bottle of wine from the rack and two glasses. "Would you care for a glass of wine while dinner is cooking?"

She nodded.

"What makes you think I have secrets?"

"Oh, I don't know. Perhaps the fact that you would have to kill me after you told me about your life and your choices." Lauren tasted the wine. "You're a wine connoisseur as well?"

He tipped his glass to hers in answer to the question.

"I started with the Secret Service after the academy and a position in Narcotics came up for an undercover assignment in Mexico to stop the drug operation out of New York. I stumbled across John's warehouse about six months ago. Last week I discovered there was a hit assigned for both of you. The Washington office said they had men in New Jersey to protect you and John. Then Kevin called a couple of days ago with the news that John had been killed. We are so close to cracking this case wide open and making arrests, but there's something or someone missing in the puzzle. There has to be someone who knows how to hide the money and invest it elsewhere. It's been hard to trace. If I can figure that out, I can make my arrests. I thought John might be the one to lead me to the main partner. Now that's impossible." Brett walked out onto the back terrace. Lauren followed and placed her hand on his back for comfort. He appeared more sad than frustrated. She wondered why. He didn't know her or her husband.

"I still can't believe John was caught up in this mess. I thought I knew my husband."

Brett turned to face her. "I was just as shocked when I first discovered John's involvement."

She wondered if he'd known John. But before she could ask, Brett gestured for Lauren to be quiet and placed his hand over her mouth. He moved in closer and whispered against her ear.

"Stay close to me. We're not alone."

She stood frozen in time and awaited his direction. She was consumed with fear. *Not again.*

Brett took her hand and slowly led her across the terrace to the steps that led to the beach. The alarm had been set, but Brett seemed to think they were not alone. She wondered if he had a sixth sense. Brett motioned for her to crawl along the side of the house toward the front. There were bushes that hugged the front corner of the house. He pointed for her to hide in behind them. Crouched down below window sight with his back against the house, he drew his gun. Lauren watched in horror. Brett tossed her back a look of reassurance, then disappeared around the corner.

****

"Don't move," Brett told the man, his gun against the man's head. He reached around and disarmed the stranger in his house. Brett quickly put the gun under the belt on his jeans and pulled the man back onto the terrace. Within seconds, Brett knocked the stranger unconscious and handcuffed him to a rail on the terrace. He re-entered his house quietly. Brett knew Mendez would have sent two men as he did to the motel. He headed upstairs slowly and discovered the other man. Brett knocked him out before the man realized what happened to him.

He heard Lauren gasp when he pulled her out of the bushes.

"Come on, we have to hurry," he told her as he dragged her toward his garage.

He knew they could no longer take Kevin's car. Brett wondered how they could have found them here. There was no one on their tail since the motel. Kevin was the only one who knew they were headed to the beach house. Brett suddenly wondered about Kevin.

Had they found him and forced it out of him? Brett needed to quickly put a plan together.

He entered through the farthest garage door. And went straight to his motorcycle covered with a tarp. He bought it before he took the assignment in Mexico. He hadn't even had a chance to take it on the road or license it. No one knew he'd purchased it. On the shelf beside the bike were two helmets, one smaller than the other. Lauren threw him a questioning look but he ignored it. He didn't have time to explain that either. She'd been right. He had secrets. Brett handed her the smaller helmet and put his on. He reached for two leather jackets that hung on the wall and helped her put one on. She asked no questions. Brett figured she must be scared and trusted him to keep her alive. Brett tried Kevin's cell with no answer. He left a message they'd been discovered. He worried that Kevin had been too. This time he didn't say where they were headed. He needed to protect Lauren. Brett took notice of a black sedan parked across from his driveway. He assumed the car belonged Mendez's men so he flattened the tires with a knife he kept in his boot. Seconds later they traveled down the shore road on his bike. Lauren held onto him tightly as tears poured relentlessly down her face.

There had been one person Brett trusted besides Kevin. He pulled into a coffee shop on the outskirts of Washington and made a call from the phone booth inside. He gestured for Lauren to have a seat in the booth beside the phone. She shook her head.

"Rick, I need your help."

"Brett? Is that you? Are you still in Mexico?"

Rick had been Brett's partner in the Secret Service. He hadn't heard from Brett since he took the undercover assignment.

"Yeah it's me. I need a place to stay for the night. " He didn't want to get into it over the phone.

"Of course partner. I'm home."

Chapter Six

"Three years and you didn't call me once." Rick stood in his driveway as Brett removed his helmet and extended his hand. The two men shook hands.

"I've been undercover," Brett explained.

Rick looked over Brett's shoulder at Lauren and then back to him with a raised eyebrow.

"Rick, this is Lauren. There's a hit out for her from Nick Mendez. Think you could put us up for the night?"

"You bet. What are partners for?" Rick walked over to Lauren and held out an arm to escort her into his home. Once inside, Rick offered them a drink.

"Something smells great," Lauren added after she thanked Rick for the drink.

"Dinner will be ready shortly. I wasn't expecting company so it's nothing elaborate," Rick informed them. Lauren remained in the living room with her drink. Brett followed Rick into the kitchen.

"So what's the deal partner?" Rick's smile referred to Lauren. Brett could read him better than anyone. They were close for a few years in the Secret Service. Rick had been there for Brett when Lisa died; another terrible tragedy that drove Brett straight into the Narcotics division. Lisa and Brett had only dated a few months but anyone could see how they were drawn to each other. Her love of motorcycles made Brett purchase one. She'd been killed in a car accident before she even got to see it. Brett was about to propose while showing her the motorcycle when she received the call about her sister. Lisa's sister had overdosed that night. She left in such a hurry she didn't give Brett time to say he'd drive. The curvy shore road, high speed and the emotional devastation on her mind took her life that night. Brett spoke to no one for a couple of weeks except Rick. Then the narcotics posting came up and Brett applied. Between his parents and Lisa, he was more than determined to stop the drug operations that had taken the three people he loved.

"There is no deal," Brett answered.

"Yeah right, buddy. I've seen that look in your eye before. She's not just an assignment is she?"

"Not now Rick, I need to keep her alive."

Brett's tone told Rick that it was not up for discussion. There were more important things to discuss. Rick respected his partner's request and changed the subject.

"How long do you think you can dodge Nick Mendez single-handed?" Rick inquired.

"Not long on my own."

Brett ran his hands through his hair in frustration and filled Rick in about the attempts on Lauren's life in the past twenty-four hours and John's death with the brief fact that he knew John in college but didn't keep in touch.

"Sounds like you got yourself in a tight spot buddy. What can I do to help?"

"My superior, Kevin Williams in the Narcotics division, is now MIA. I saw him this afternoon to switch cars about fifty miles from my place and now I'm not sure where he is. He's the only one that knew we were headed to my beach house. Can you look into his disappearance for me?"

Rick handed the stir spoon to Brett and motioned for him to take care of the sauce.

"You stir. I'm going to begin a trace on Kevin's phone."

While Brett stirred the sauce and thought about what to do next, Lauren entered the kitchen.

"Brett, I know you told me there was no contact allowed and I've trusted you so far to keep me alive, but we're running out of options. I called my father. He's sending the private jet that will take me to a safe place until this is all over. It's best. I know you have a case to close and arrests to make. I'm just in your way and it appears I'm taking up your time that would be best put to making those arrests."

"What!" Brett dropped the spoon and sauce splattered across the kitchen floor.

Rick ran into the kitchen.

"Is everything okay in here?" Rick asked cautiously.

"No, it's not," Brett announced sarcastically and stormed into the living room.

Rick looked at Lauren and she simply shrugged her shoulders. He followed his friend and motioned his arms in the air. Brett ignored him and changed the subject.

"Did you find any trace of Kevin?"

"His phone is turned off or has become obsolete."

Brett worried it was the latter.

"I've traced the vehicle's FBI GPS to an abandoned warehouse on the east side. Up for a little investigation my friend? That is if your little domestic dispute is finished." Rick chuckled.

"It's not a domestic dispute. She called her father against my orders. I said no contact. Apparently daddy's jet is on its way to get her."

"What do we do with her?" Rick asked.

"We take her with us for now."

Brett walked into the kitchen, turned the stove off and grabbed Lauren by the arm.

"You're coming with us now."

"I told you my father's jet is on its way!"

Lauren tried to struggle free from Brett's hold but was unsuccessful as they passed Rick on their way to the front door. Rick grabbed his keys and remained quiet.

"Daddy can wait. My job is to keep you alive. That means you stay with me."

Rick drove while Brett sat in the backseat with Lauren. She didn't speak. She sat and looked out the window. Rick filled Brett in on the warehouse. He had quickly looked at the blueprints he brought up on his computer so he would know all entrances. The warehouse had been abandoned for years and there were no apparent crimes in or around it since it sat empty.

Rick turned off the car lights as they entered the gravel road that led up to the warehouse. There were no lights on or around the warehouse except for a few dimly lit street lights, and no signs of anyone within the vicinity. As they drove closer to the warehouse, Brett noticed the car. He confirmed to Rick that it was the one he had switched with Kevin. They pulled up beside it and Brett got out and searched the car. He came back to Rick's window and informed him it was empty and there was no sign of foul play.

"Let's check inside the warehouse." Brett opened the back door and motioned for Lauren to get out.

"I'm not going in there. It might be dangerous!" She crossed her arms.

Brett reached in and pulled her out of the car. "You think it's safer to stay here without me?"

"You really want to throw me into a possible line of fire?" Lauren barked at him.

"No. I want to keep you alive. You're safer with me. Now shut-up and come on."

Rick kept quiet. He definitely didn't want to get into the middle of this one. But he knew Brett was right. She had to stay with them.

Brett motioned to the door beyond Kevin's car. He kept one hand on Lauren's arm and forced her behind him. He drew his gun and flashlight with the other hand and stayed to one side of the door. Rick drew his gun and flashlight too, and then reached for the door handle. It was unlocked and he opened it quickly. Brett went in first with Lauren behind him and Rick followed. There wasn't a sound or sign of anyone present in the warehouse. They walked down a darkened corridor into the open abandoned warehouse. It was then they heard a sound. It was Lauren's shriek. Brett quickly put his hand over her mouth to quiet her. She nodded to Brett. She began to shake. Brett's flashlight gave them enough light to show a man hanging in the middle of the warehouse, a stool knocked over below the hung man. It would appear the man had taken his own life. Brett knew better. It was a staged death. One that Nick Mendez was famous for but never proven. Brett let go of Lauren and walked toward the man. It was indeed Kevin. Rigor mortis had already set in.

"Sorry buddy." Rick patted Brett's shoulder.

"How could I have missed someone on our tail?" Brett wondered aloud.

"It happens to the best of us Brett, don't beat yourself up," Rick encouraged his friend.

"She's probably safer with *daddy*." Brett stressed his last word and turned to Lauren who was far enough away not to hear him.

"It's an option but I think you should go with her. She's safer in your hands," Rick suggested strongly.

Brett looked at Rick, "Maybe you're right. I've run out of options. Perhaps her father has a safe place to buy some time to get my head straight."

Brett took Lauren by the arm and led her out of the warehouse.

"Where are we going now? What about Kevin? You can't just leave him."

Lauren rambled and Brett ignored her questions. He opened the back door to Rick's car and motioned for her to get in. He may have appeared cold and emotionless to her, but he had too much on his mind. He couldn't think straight. She definitely had become a distraction. He knew he had to focus to keep her alive. He knew he had to bury the feelings he felt for her. The only option left was the one he had refused since the beginning. He turned around to Lauren.

"We're going to meet your father's jet. My job is to keep you safe and alive. I'm coming with you."

Lauren just sat quietly and nodded.

Rick stopped at his office on the way to the airport. He handed Brett an untraceable phone so they could keep in touch. Rick informed Brett he would continue to help him solve the case.

The Vanderholm jet waited on a private runway for them. Once Rick stopped the car, Lauren quickly jumped out and ran into her father's arms.

"You've got your hands full. Don't worry buddy, I'll help you crack this."

Rick waved good-bye as Brett walked toward Lauren and her father.

"Charles Vanderholm" Lauren's father extended his hand.

"Agent Brent Donovan"

Brett announced and looked Charles straight in the eye. Brett still had his doubts about the man's involvement. Now he had one more life to protect while he figured out who was hiding Nick Mendez's drug money.

"Lauren filled me in briefly. I still can't believe my son-in-law was involved with this. Are you certain, Agent?"

"Yes, sir, I am." Brett's tone held no hesitation.

"Thank you for keeping her safe, but I can take it from here."

Charles' words sounded more like an order than respect. Brett thought of his father for a moment. He chuckled to himself. The two men were so alike.

"I'll be joining you, sir. Lauren is still in my protective custody," Brett told him and without hesitation led Lauren to the stairs of the jet.

Charles did not look impressed. Charles said nothing and entered the jet. After the jet took off, Charles excused himself.

"I'll be in my office. The staff aboard the jet will take care of any need."

Brett looked at Lauren after Charles left them.

"That's about the extent of the time we spend together. Business has always been more important." Lauren's tone spoke loud and clear. Brett didn't remark. He knew personally what she meant. His father had been the same. Lauren grabbed a pillow and reclined her chair. She looked completely relaxed. Brett felt differently. Something in Charles's eyes told him the man was not to be trusted. He didn't trust this man to keep Lauren safe. Brett got up quietly and did not stir Lauren. He walked down the aisle and noticed the staff busy in the kitchenette preparing a light snack. He moved further down the aisle and stood outside Charles's office door and listened.

****

"Yes Nick, I have my daughter. The man with her is Agent Brett Donovan with the FBI Narcotics division. My daughter confirmed the agent told her of John's connection to you, his death wasn't an accident and you have a hit out for her. I have a lot at stake here. Finish the job."

Charles heard a dial tone and pressed the End button. For a long moment he sat and stared at the files on his desk.

Chapter Seven

Brett returned to his seat next to Lauren without a word. His instincts were right. *How the hell do I tell Lauren her father is the missing link and wants her dead?* Brett hoped she would sleep. He needed to come up with a plan before they landed.

Brett messaged Rick to dig deep into Charles Vanderholm and his financial records. He informed him that Charles was the missing link. Brett knew they were not headed for a safe place and asked Rick to place a track on his phone. He knew he could trust Rick. That thought made him think of Kevin. Kevin had been his only contact outside of the drug world for three years. Their brief but few chats kept Brett going. Kevin was not only his superior but also a trusted friend. Brett had no choice but to leave Kevin in that warehouse. He couldn't risk blowing this case. He had given up his life to bring down Nick Mendez and his New York operations.

How the hell is a father capable of ordering his own daughter's death? He rubbed his hand across his jaw. His father had been obsessed with the family business and had never forgiven Brett for his choices but he knew his father couldn't put out a hit on his own child. Beyond frustrated, his fist hit the table in front of him. He looked up to find Charles beside him with a stern look on his face.

"What's wrong?"

"You tell me Mr. Vanderholm," Brett said, in an accusing tone.

Lauren stirred from her sleep.

"Tell you what, Agent?"

"Why you ordered your daughter's death?" Brett drew his gun.

Lauren jumped from her seat.

"Brett, have you lost your mind?"

She went to move toward her father, but Brett held her back.

"Well, Mr. Vanderholm, are you going to explain why you just made a phone call to Nick Mendez informing him of Lauren's whereabouts and that you demand he finish the job?"

Brett's tone grew louder with each word as he demanded answers.

Lauren looked confused. She glanced back and forth between her father and Brett.

Charles calmly took a seat. He appeared completely relaxed as though he'd done nothing wrong.

"Agent Donovan, I have no contact with this Nick Mendez. I only know the name because my daughter told me this was the man connected to John's death and the attempts on her life. It is extremely rude to listen to another's conversation. You have assumed without asking who I spoke to in my private office."

He sat back and continued with confidence.

"If you must know, I was on the phone with my lawyer. I always inform him of any potential threat to the family business or name. And for finishing a job that was regular business talk. Business must continue even under circumstances such as this."

Charles did not flinch. The tone of his voice remained confident, yet Brett was trained to detect lies. This time he was certain Charles was covering his ass. He looked back at Lauren.

"Yes, my father's lawyer's name is Nick. Satisfied?"

There was anger in Lauren's eyes as she pushed past Brett to join her father. He knew he had to regain her trust in order to protect her. At the moment it was his word against her father's. Brett knew what he had heard and Charles's exact words.

Brett took a quick breath and held out his hand. "I'm sorry Mr. Vanderholm. My assignment is to protect your daughter at all costs."

Charles stood and shook Brett's extended hand.

"I respect a man with integrity. We're on the same side. We both want Lauren safe."

Charles gave his daughter a barely-there hug and announced his return to his office until they landed.

"May I ask where we are going, sir?"

Charles turned with a solemn look.

"Our summer home in The Hamptons; enjoy the light lunch provided by the staff. We land in a half-hour."

Without another word, Charles retreated to his office. Brett had to come up with a plan. His only help was Rick. Lauren kept to the opposite side of the plane without a word to Brett. He knew damn well she was pissed at him for the accusation. Brett messaged Rick their destination and a request for back-up.

A limo waited for them on the airstrip. Lauren walked with her father. Brett followed. An uneasy feeling stirred in his gut. No one spoke on the short ride to the summer estate in East Hampton. Brett took note of the quiet neighborhood. Though they arrived late at night Brett still assumed it to be quiet during daylight hours. Most homes here were only used in the summer months. Brett wondered if this was the reason Charles chose the summer home. The silence in the limo broke when they stopped in front of an elegant estate.

"I'm sorry Lauren, but there will be no staff at the home. The earliest I could arrange for staff is tomorrow afternoon."

"Will you be staying?" Lauren asked her father.

"No. I have business in New York I must attend to. I'm sure Agent Donovan will protect you."

Brett heard a touch of sarcasm in Charles's tone. His gut told him that Charles didn't even care if his daughter would be protected. Charles remained in the limo. Lauren waved good-bye to her father and walked toward the front door. Brett made eye contact with Charles but didn't speak, then stepped out of the car and closed the limo door. *What a cold man* . He followed Lauren. He hoped Rick found proof of the connection between Charles and the Mendez family. Then he had to convince Lauren and get her away from the home where she felt safe.

Brett walked into money. He thought *his* family had left him a substantial inheritance. He stood in amazement. His sports bag dropped to the floor. Lauren stopped before she climbed the staircase and turned.

"A little overwhelming at first but it's a beautiful home. I desperately need a long soak in the tub. Make yourself at home."

Her tone remained cold. His job to convince her of her father's involvement with the Mendez family would be difficult. Brett grabbed the piece of paper from his pocket. Charles handed him the alarm codes before he left the limo. After he set the alarm he picked up his bag and began his search for a drink.

****

Lauren turned on the water and lit a few candles. She removed the clothes from the second-hand store and tossed them in the laundry hamper. She wondered if she should burn them. Then she looked at the shoes she'd just taken off. Never in her lifetime did she think she'd wear flip-flops. But Brett was right about their comfort. That thought only made her think of Brett and the past couple of days with him. The one heated night they shared. Then she remembered his accusation that her father wanted her dead. Lauren stepped into her bath and sunk into the bubbles. The warm water surrounded her body and began to relax. Her eyes closed. She thought of Brett and their night in that run-down motel. Then she remembered her guilt afterward. She should be mourning her husband not crawling into bed with a stranger. So much confusion raced through her thoughts. Her sadness for the loss of her husband, her feelings for Brett she tried hard to deny and the fear for her life.

The water cooled and the bubbles dissolved. Still confused, Lauren stepped out and reached for her robe. She sat at her dressing table and brushed her hair. She swept it up into a French-twist and applied a touch of make-up. Lauren dressed in black silk top and matching silk shorts. She wanted to crawl into bed and hide under the blanket like she did as a child when she'd just had a nightmare. Her stomach told her not to. She slept on the jet and missed the food prepared for her. She knew she wouldn't be able to sleep anyway so she decided to head to the kitchen. She took the west wing staircase at the end of the hallway that led straight into the kitchen. She hoped she didn't run into Brett. She wasn't ready to talk to him.

"How was your soak in the tub?" Brett asked as she entered the kitchen.

Damn! Why didn't I just crawl into bed? "Fine," Lauren answered quickly.

She knew the one-word-answer seemed cold. She sighed heavily.

"Sorry. I don't mean to sound rude. I'm just tired, scared and angry."

"You have every right to feel that way, Lauren. There's a hit out for you and I've accused your father of being involved."

Brett dipped the spoon he held into the sauce. He stepped closer to her.

"This may help. Honestly, I am one hell of a chef. One that has promised to feed you a couple of times now."

He smiled. The smell drifted into her senses and drove her stomach wild. She took the offering and smiled. The taste aroused her senses and she forgot her recent thoughts.

"I take that as a yes?" Brett inquired.

"Perfect. I'm starving."

Brett poured her a glass of wine and escorted her to the table.

"Your dinner will be served momentarily."

Lauren appeased her hunger with a few bites before she broke the silence.

"Brett?" Her tone called out question time.

He set his fork down and looked up.

"Yes."

"What makes you think my father is involved? I know he's not the loving devoted father, but I'm sure he wouldn't want me dead. That's just absurd."

Brett sighed. "I know what I heard outside his door. I can recite the exact words to you. If you still believe he was speaking with his lawyer, then maybe I'm wrong. Still. I'm waiting for Rick to get back to me with information to prove it."

"What were his exact words?" Lauren asked him.

She needed to know. She thought her father loved her but she knew business always came first. Brett reached for her hand. His thumb rubbed the top of it as he looked into her eyes and conveyed what he heard, word-for-word. Lauren gasped. She pulled her hand from Brett's and stood. She walked into the sitting area off the kitchen and collapsed into the leather chair in front of the fireplace.

Brett followed her.

"I'm sorry Lauren. I played along with your father's version of the phone call he supposedly had with his lawyer. I want him to think I believe him. We're not safe here."

He knelt down before her.

Her eyes filled with tears of sadness but mostly of fear.

"Do you really believe my father wants to have me killed?"

Brett nodded. She didn't want to believe her father was capable of this. She trusted him.

"He wants me dead for the sake of his business, his name?"

"I'm afraid so Lauren."

"He had my husband killed?" Lauren asked Brett through tears.

"I believe John wanted out. One doesn't walk away from Mendez business. You're just part of the cleanup in case John told you anything." Brett wiped her tears with his thumbs.

"And how is my father involved?"

"From what I overheard, I now believe your father is the missing link. I've tried to uncover the Mendez connection to who laundered the drug money. John's warehouse may have been used the past few years to move drugs but there had to be somebody with enough power and money to hide the funds in an overseas account. Rick is going to search your father's accounts. Then we will have our proof. For now I need you to continue to play along. Should your father call you, you need to talk to him as if I've told you none of this. Can you do this for me Lauren?"

Lauren sat quietly and tried to absorb what Brett just told her. She nodded. She knew she had no other choice. She believed Brett would protect her and keep her from harm. She knew her father would never call anyway.

"I know it's a lot to digest Lauren. Trust me. I will keep you safe." Brett's hand touched her cheek softly.

Lauren looked into his eyes. She hoped he'd keep her safe. At this point she wasn't sure who to trust.

"I'm scared. Will you stay with me in my room? I don't want to be alone in this big house." Lauren asked.

Brett nodded and took her hand. He grabbed his phone and gun from the table on their way through the kitchen.

Chapter Eight

"You're wearing the flip-flops?" Brett laughed as he followed Lauren up the stairs. A slight chuckle came with her answer which pleased him. Through all the horrific news and experiences the past few days, he smiled.

"You are right. They are comfortable."

Lauren stopped at the top of the staircase. "Brett, am I going to die?"

The fear in her eyes ripped at his heart. He swallowed hard.

"Not with me around. May I ask one favor of you?"

"Anything"

The desperation in her tone only convinced him he needed to remain focused.

"Could you put on something more…uh…less appealing?" He stumbled with the last couple of words then laughed.

She looked down at her silk camisole and shorts and then laughed.

"Sorry. I'll throw on some sweats. They'll go great with the flip-flops."

Brett laughed through a thank you.

She continued on into her bedroom and to her bathroom.

"We still haven't talked about that night in the motel."

Lauren called out from behind the bathroom door.

He didn't answer.

She opened the door and stood in sweats as she promised.

"Better?" she asked.

Even in sweats, his heart raced. It didn't seem to make any difference to him. He still wanted her. He'd ignored her comment about the other night but it had never left his thoughts. Brett smiled.

"Not really."

Lauren said nothing. She moved closer to him and removed the sweats. She stood a mere two inches away from him, totally naked.

"Is this better?" she whispered.

His tongue moved across his bottom lip. He felt his jeans tighten.

"I surrender every part of me to you."

The seductive smile that followed her comment made him speechless.

"No comment Agent Donovan? Should I continue to talk or are you going to shut me up?"

He answered that by pressing his lips against hers instantly. His hunger for her passionately unraveled and he deepened the kiss. Her hands roamed over the taut denim that barely contained him. He groaned lightly through the kiss. Her hands traveled to the waistline of his jeans and pulled his shirt out. He felt her hands move upward to his chest. He twitched from her touch and moved in closer to her. Brett's rough hands rested on her lower back and held her tight against him. Their kiss paused as she pulled his shirt over his head and tossed it to the floor. Her bare breasts pushed against his chest. He felt her heart beat against his. The desperate hunger he saw in her eyes pleaded for his lips. His tongue traced the outline of her bottom lip and she reached for his belt. Her action made him nibble on her lip. As she undid his zipper and released his restriction, his tongue delved into the depths of her mouth. The grasp her mouth had on his tongue heightened his arousal and he swept her into his arms. Gently he laid her on the bed and joined her. His focus to keep his mind on the assignment to protect her had completely disappeared.

Their bodies lay tangled in the sheets, exhausted after their passion overcame them. Reality entered Brett's mind as he thought about his first priority to protect Lauren at all costs. He knew he had to remain focused on his job and not his desires or she could end up dead.

"Lauren," he whispered.

No response. He turned his head to see her fast asleep. Frustrated, he slid out of bed without disturbing her. He searched for his jeans and his gun before he headed to the bathroom. The silence in the house grew eerie. He didn't turn on the bathroom light and left the bathroom door open an inch or two. The moonlight gave enough light for him. He didn't want to stir Lauren. If anything she deserved some rest in her own bed. He reached for the zipper of his jean when a noise in the distance stopped him. He reached for his gun and slid up against the wall beside the door. The crack in the open door allowed him to slowly lean toward it to have a look. He saw a dark shadow carry Lauren's limp body out of the bedroom. Brett opened the door slowly and crept toward the bedroom door. His hands firmly held his gun while he peered out into the hall. The dark figure climbed down the stairs with Lauren's body. Brett wondered if she had been drugged. She hadn't woken or screamed. He entered the hall and moved toward the staircase. The shadowed figure stopped at the front foyer and set Lauren down on the floor. Brett pointed his gun directly at the shadow. This was the perfect opportunity to take him out as Lauren lay safely out of gun fire range. Brett called out as the shadow reached for the door handle.

"Stop and put your hands where I can see them," Brett ordered.

Before he fired, the front door swung open hard and knocked the man to the floor. From the outside light, Brett saw Rick with his gun drawn. Brett raced down the stairs to Lauren. Rick already had the man on the floor in cuffs.

"Perfect timing partner," Brett announced as he picked Lauren up off the floor.

Lauren moaned, "What happened?"

"You're safe. Your father allowed Mendez to send someone to finish the job. Fortunately, they did not succeed."

Brett carried her into the nearby room and wrapped her in a blanket. She smiled and closed her eyes. Brett gently placed her on the sofa and attended to the fireplace. He wanted her close and warm.

Rick cleared his throat. "What do you want me to do with this?"

Rick tossed the masked man into a chair.

Brett pulled the mask off. He didn't recognize him.

"Who sent you? Mendez?" Brett demanded.

The man shook his head.

"Charles Vanderholm?" Brett placed his hand around the man's windpipe. He tightened his grip and the man finally nodded.

Rick added, "Her father really wants her dead. That's just sad."

Brett let go of the man and looked over at Rick, "And I thought my father was bad."

"I searched records for bank transactions and this is what I found." Rick dug into his pocket and pulled out a piece of paper. He handed it to Brett.

Brett looked over at Lauren asleep on the sofa and then Rick.

"The overseas account connected to Mendez is in Lauren's name?"

Brett gave Rick a puzzled look.

"I imagine it's a cover. Poor girl probably doesn't even know she has the account," Rick commented.

"That son-of-a-bitch"

Brett's loud tone stirred Lauren and he turned when she called out his name. She started to get up and realized she had nothing on under the blanket. She wrapped it tighter around her body and stood with a horrified look in her eyes.

"What the hell just happened?" She stormed across the room and demanded an answer.

"She's a fiery one," Rick quietly spoke.

Brett nodded. "Lauren, calm down. You're safe now. Your father sent someone to kill you."

Before Lauren could get another word out the man cuffed to the chair spoke up.

"I wasn't sent to kill her. Just take her to the safe place."

His sudden outburst jolted Brett.

Lauren turned to the man. "My father doesn't want me dead?"

He nodded in agreement.

"Makes sense," Rick interrupted. "If he wanted her dead, the job would have been done. He wouldn't have drugged her to get her out of the house."

Rick's words confirmed Brett's question of why the man tried to take Lauren out of the house drugged.

Lauren snapped at Brett. "See, I knew my father wouldn't want me dead."

Brett handed her the piece of paper in his hand.

"But he seemed to be more interested in saving his own ass to put yours in jeopardy."

Lauren read the paper. "Business always comes first before family."

She didn't appear shocked her father had set her up to take the fall. She tossed the paper on the sofa and stormed up the stairs.

Brett ran his hand through his messed hair. He sighed with frustration. Part of him wanted to run after her and part of him told him to stay the hell away. He'd already done enough damage. He lost focus on his assignment to protect her. It almost cost her life.

Chapter Nine

Lauren slammed the bedroom door and then froze. She looked at the tangled sheets on the bed, not sure what she felt. There were so many emotions racing through her veins. She knew in her heart she had fallen for him but her anger continued to ignore it. He was there to protect her from her own father. Yet the recent discovery that her father tried to protect her from the Mendez family touched her heart. Until she remembered the piece of paper Brett showed her. She didn't know who to trust anymore. Her emotions were all over the map. And at a time she should be grieving the loss of her husband. Her fiery temper took control and she picked up the phone to give her father a piece of her mind.

"Lauren? Are you okay?" The tone in his voice almost sounded concerned.

"I'm fine, *Daddy*," Lauren stressed the last word sarcastically.

"What's wrong?" Charles asked as if he didn't already know.

"What's wrong? You need to ask! Why are you involved with this drug family? Are you the reason John is dead?"

One question hurled out of her mouth after another. She didn't give her father a chance to answer.

"And, what's this about an overseas account in my name that's connected to the Mendez family? You save your own ass Daddy to allow me to take the fall?"

Lauren's tone grew frantic. She knew her father always allowed business to come first but this had drawn the line.

The line went quiet. Charles did not or could not answer his daughter. She slammed the receiver down hard and stormed into her closet to get dressed.

Now the time had come to set things straight with Brett. She no longer wanted him there to protect her. She trusted him about as much as she trusted her father at the moment. She had enough money to buy the protection she needed once her father cleared her name from any connection to the Mendez family. Lauren stopped at the top of the staircase. She could hear Brett and Rick talk from the room off the front foyer. She stood still and listened.

"Brett, stop it. She's alive. That's the assignment. There's enough evidence to arrest Nick Mendez for money laundering. That alone will keep his lawyers busy for some time."

"Money laundering is not what I'm after him for. I want his drugs off our streets. This man needs to be put behind bars for the rest of his life. Do you know how many people he's killed with and without his drugs?"

"Well, unless you get Charles Vanderholm to confess, you won't get him on murder. There's not even enough circumstantial evidence there."

"That bastard frames his daughter to save his own ass, besides the fact that he didn't stop the hit on John."

"I know you're hurting, man. Mendez has taken everyone you ever cared for—your parents, your fiancée and your best friend."

"If John had only reached out to me, I could have helped him."

Lauren cleared her throat. Her presence seemed to startle the men.

"John was your best friend? You knew the guilt I carried once I slept with you. I should have been mourning my husband instead of jumping in bed with a stranger. Now you tell me, I slept with his best friend."

Before Brett could explain it to her, she looked at Rick, "I want Agent Donovan removed from this assignment. I would like you to protect me until this matter is cleared."

Without a word, she spun on her heels and went back upstairs.

Lauren threw herself onto her bed in tears. She swore she would never trust another man as long as she lived. Through her own hurt she realized how much her mother would suffer from this news. Her world would be turned upside down. Lauren sat up on the bed and wiped her tears. She needed to deal with the matter at hand now, her father. She knew she had to be strong for her mother. Lauren regained her composure and waited for Rick to take her to her parents' home in New Jersey.

****

"She didn't know you and John were friends?" Rick waited until he heard the upstairs door slam. The past hour had been dramatic and he felt bad for Brett. He could read Brett like an open book. Brett had feelings for Lauren, whether he wanted to admit it or not.

"The right time hadn't come to explain how I knew John back in college. Things happened that shouldn't have. I lost focus, Rick and it almost cost her life."

The doorbell rang and Rick left the room to answer the door to four FBI agents. Two of them announced they were there to transport the suspect in custody. The other two for Lauren's protection. Brett spoke up and said he had to grab his bag upstairs and he'd go with the agents and the suspect. Rick placed his hand on Brett's chest and stopped him from going upstairs.

"I think it's best if I gather your belongings."

Brett nodded.

Rick knocked gently on the door.

"Yes," Lauren answered.

"I've come to get Brett's stuff. Can I come in?"

She told him to come in. He entered to find her pointing to the black bag on the floor. It had a shirt and jacket tossed on top of it.

"Everything of his is there," Lauren coldly announced. "Let me know when he's gone and we're ready to go. I need to go to my parents' house. This news is going to destroy my mother. I hope you will join me, Rick."

Rick nodded. Unsure of what else to say he mentioned he'd be back when they were ready to leave. Lauren thanked him politely.

Rick handed Brett his bag. Brett tossed his shirt and jacket on. He reached out to shake Rick's hand, "Keep her safe."

"I will buddy. I'll be in touch."

Chapter Ten

Lauren drew in a deep breath as the car pulled up to her parents' home. There were already two FBI vehicles parked with flashing lights. Her heart ached for her mother. She jumped out of the car and ran to the front door. Rick followed and flashed his badge to allow Lauren and him to enter the home. She spotted her mother in the sitting room and rushed to her side. She embraced her warmly. Her mother's first concern touched her heart.

"Are you all right, my sweetheart?" Marion gently brushed her daughter's hair away from her face.

"I'm fine, Mom. I'm more worried about you. I wish I arrived before the FBI showed up."

Lauren watched her mother's eyes drift toward the front door and she turned. Her father walked toward the front door, in handcuffs, escorted by two FBI men. He looked their way momentarily and then lowered his head. She wondered if he felt any remorse for anything he'd done. Lauren heard her mother's cries and turned to comfort her.

"He does have the best attorneys," Lauren whispered in her mother's ear. She didn't know what else to say to comfort her mother.

Her mom withdrew from their embrace. The cold expression frightened Lauren.

"He killed your husband and agreed to have you killed. I never want to see him again."

Lauren watched her mother stand, straighten her skirt and walk up the stairs with poise and confidence. Sadness settled in her heart instead of anger. Her father lost everything he built because of greed. Business definitely came before family.

****

Charles sat in a small, cold and dingy room at the Newark FBI headquarters, what felt like forever. Not one agent had come in to question him. Nor had anyone come to ask if he'd like a cup of coffee or anything for that matter. He realized he'd lost everything. He'd been arrested for money-laundering with the records Rick uncovered, but not yet officially charged. He worried the charge of conspiracy to murder might be next along with the drug connection to the Mendez family. For the first time, Charles Vanderholm was not calm and no longer in control. Business always came first. His name and reputation depended on it. Now even that was gone. He knew his business would never recover the accusations let alone the charges about to be brought against him. Sweat dripped from his brow, he fidgeted with his hands and his knees shook underneath the table as he awaited his fate.

The sound the door made when it opened made Charles practically jump out of his skin.

"Mr. Vanderholm, we meet again." Brett closed the door and tossed a folder on the table.

"Thank you for protecting my daughter," he said in a shaky voice.

"As if you care about your daughter's well-being, you son-of-a-bitch!"

Brett pulled the chair out from the table and took a seat. The chair legs scratched against the old floor and made Charles twitch.

"A little nervous I see. You should be. Let's see…"

Brett opened the folder briefly and looked at Charles.

"So far we have you for money-laundering. I might add how pathetic to put your own daughter's name on the account. There's also conspiracy to murder and the connection to the Mendez family. Did I forget anything?" Brett smiled.

"I have never dealt drugs. I tried to save my daughter."

Charles squirmed in his chair and tried to display confidence. The continuous bead of sweat that formed on his brow made it impossible.

"Did I mention drugs? I don't think so."

Brett scratched his head and looked at the file.

There were a few moments of silence which made Charles uncomfortable. He figured this was

Brett's method to get a confession. Charles never enjoyed games.

"What is it you want, Agent Donovan? I'm not into game-playing here."

Charles leaned forward and crossed his cuffed-hands on the table. Brett pointed to the cuffs.

"To me, it doesn't appear this conversation is in your favor, Charles."

Brett starred directly into his eyes. Charles took a deep breath and leaned back in his chair.

"I need answers. If you are helpful, maybe there's something we can do for you."

Brett appeared to make an offer which puzzled Charles. He figured the Agent wanted to take down Nick Mendez and an opportunity presented itself to weasel out of this mess.

"What do you want from me? And what do I get out of it?" Charles's interest grew.

Brett stood up and walked to the door. He turned and calmly stood. His hand grazed across his unshaved chin.

"Testify against Nick Mendez for the drug deals through John's warehouse, the laundering of the drug money and of course, John's murder and the attempted murder of Lauren. That's your offer."

Brett opened the door, "I'll give you some time to think it over."

"I may as well sign a death order." Charles spoke up.

Brett held the door open.

"The FBI is willing to give you witness protection with house-arrest."

"Does my family come with me?" Charles asked.

"I don't believe your family would want to."

Brett closed the door and left Charles alone to contemplate the offer.

Charles wondered how long they'd leave him alone this time.

An hour later, Brett entered the room again where Charles sat and pondered his choices.

"Well?" Brett remained standing.

"I'll sign whatever you want, but I would like to talk to my wife and daughter first."

He knew they'd never go into witness protection with him, but he wanted to apologize for the mess he put them in. For the first time in his life, he thought of his wife and daughter.

"I'll see if they'll come. I can't guarantee it." Brett left the room again.

Fifteen minutes later Brett returned. His solemn expression told Charles what he already knew. His family would not come. He didn't blame them. He'd lost everything and was about to sign his death notice.

Nick Mendez would have him killed before he could testify. The FBI could not protect him.

"They won't come?" Charles asked.

Brett nodded and Charles lowered his head.

Brett tossed a pad of paper and a pen on the table.

"Write your statement in your own words. Once you're done. We will video-tape your confession." Brett left the room.

Normally, Charles would have had a team of lawyers present. He refused his right to call his lawyer. Defeated and scared, he picked up the pen. The FBI agents who'd arrested Charles at his home entered shortly after he finished. One agent set up the video equipment while the other joined Charles at the table.

"Is there anything you need before we begin?" The agent politely asked.

Charles shook his head. He confessed to his business connection with Nick Mendez for several years, the hits put out by Mendez for his son-in-law and daughter and confirmed the transportation of drugs.

"In the safe, you will find recorded conversation I had with Nick Mendez. The conversations are in regard to the transport of drugs through my son-in-law's warehouse and also one that confirms he had John Reynolds killed. There is also a folder which contains photographs of Nick Mendez and John Reynolds at the warehouse with the drugs and also bank statements to trace the laundered drug money."

Charles leaned back in his chair and watched the agent turn off the video equipment. Once they left the room, Charles knew what he had to do. He knew he'd never live long enough to testify in court. The FBI had his confession and testimony. He'd lost everything. His family wanted nothing more to do with him. Charles knew there wouldn't be much time before the agents came back to officially charge him. He slowly removed his tie and stood on his chair.

Chapter Eleven

Four Months Later – Valentine's Day
"The movers will be there at eight o'clock in the morning."

Lauren confirmed the time to her mother.

"Thank you sweetheart, I don't know what I would have done without you these past months."

After the private funeral for her father, Lauren's mother confessed she had most of her family trust fund invested outside of her husband's money. Her mother may have portrayed the obedient corporate wife, but she'd definitely outsmarted her husband for years. The arranged marriage had remained loveless except in the public eye. To the outside world, the Vanderholms were the perfect corporate couple. Lauren respected her mother for the role she'd played her entire married life. To discover her mother's wise decision to invest her family's money separate from her father's, only made her respect her more. Once her mother shared this information with her, she no longer worried. She knew her mother would be fine on her own.

"Mom, you're the strongest woman I've ever known. I think it's the other way around. I don't know what I'd do without you."

Lauren embraced her mom in a loving hug.

"I still believe you were wrong about that agent."

Brett had respected Lauren's wishes and stayed away. Her mother talked about him on their travels. After the funeral, Lauren suggested they visit her mother's sister in England and travel Europe afterward. Her mother agreed with her daughter. Lauren thought it best to stay away during the arrest and trial of Nick Mendez. The news of her father's involvement and suicide would settle and become old news. She told Lauren it was written all over her face that she loved him and that you can't just close your heart. Lauren continued to tell her it wasn't that simple.

"Please don't mention his name again, Mom."

Lauren mixed them a drink. For the past week since they arrived home from Europe, they hadn't stopped. Her father's business and estate had been secured throughout the trial. Everything had been lost. His business had been picked through with a fine-tooth comb by the FBI as they discovered his investments all tied in with the Mendez family. The FBI had allowed them back in the house to pack personal items and family heirlooms from her mother's side of the family. The movers were scheduled for the next morning to move her mother's belongings to the city. Her mother bought an exquisite flat on Park Avenue. Lauren decided she would sell her house and move to the city to be close to her mother. The time had come to leave the suburbs and the memories behind.

Lauren handed her mother a drink when the doorbell rang.

"I wonder who that could be." Lauren looked at her mother.

No one had come by since they returned from Europe. They hadn't kept in touch with anyone. Then again, their friends were mostly business acquaintances.

"Maybe it's that nice-looking agent." Her mother turned and winked.

The gesture surprised Lauren. She had never seen her mother imply anything improper.

"Mother" Lauren rolled her eyes.

"What? I'm not just your mother, Lauren. I'm also human." She snickered at her own comment.

"I'm just a little surprised," Lauren laughed.

She shook her head and opened the door, only to be surprised once more. Her mother had been right.

"Agent, what brings you here?"

He stood with a look of desperation in his eyes. Lauren's eyes travelled to the single rose held in his hand and then the trail of roses behind him.

"You"

"What's all this for?" She smiled.

Her heart began to beat faster. To see him only made her realize life without him had been lonely. Her stubbornness wouldn't allow her to admit it. She ran away and tried to close off her heart with the excuse she didn't want to leave her mother.

He reached for the bag beside him and handed it to her.

"A peace offering, I believe I made you remove these while we were on the run."

She looked in the bag to find the Chanel pantsuit and her heels. She laughed and looked down at her feet. She stood in the flip-flops.

He laughed. "I thought you didn't do flip-flops."

"I do now."

They both laughed. She knew he'd remember what he said to her at that second-hand store.

"They are comfortable for the feet."

Lauren smiled and then finally admitted the real reason.

"They remind me of you."

She met his stare. Her heart melted. Her mother was right. She did love this man.

"May I come in Lauren?"

"Do you have something to tell me that I don't want to hear?"

She remembered the first time she'd opened the door to him.

"No." He laughed. "I hope I have something to tell you that you do want to hear."

His answer intrigued her and she motioned for him to come in. Her mother met them by the door. Marion formally introduced herself to Brett and thanked him for protecting her daughter, then turned to Lauren.

"I will leave you kids to talk."

"Mom, you don't have to leave."

"Yes, I do. I'd like to get back to the city before its dark. I'll talk with you tomorrow. Remember what your mother told you."

She kissed her daughter's cheek and smiled at Brett.

****

"May I offer you a drink Agent Donovan?"

He followed her into the Cigar Room, "Only if you call me Brett."

She turned and smiled. A smile that definitely told him it pleased her to see him.

"I like to see you smile, Lauren, although you are unbelievably sexy when you're all fired up."

He winked and smiled.

She mixed them a drink and met him by the fireplace. She stood before him, eye-to-eye.

"This feels like Deja-vu."

Brett smiled. "I remember the first night we met. You were upset with me that night. You don't seem upset now."

"I'm not."

She exhaled and walked to the sofa. He followed.

"Is there possibly a chance of forgiveness?" He wondered.

"Possibly" She moved a little closer to him. He felt the heat between them. He knew he could never live without her. He cleared his throat to maintain his composure. He had something to tell her.

"Good."

He felt confident he could tell her why he had come.

"Lauren."

He set their drinks down and held her hand.

"I love you. I have since that first night. I thought it was wrong. You were my assignment. You were John's wife. You just buried him. I had to protect you. I had to bring down the Mendez family. There were so many obstacles in the way but the one thing that never got in the way was the way I felt about you."

Brett slowly lowered to one knee.

"I've been lost without you. I lived for the chase, the danger. You were right. I was addicted to it. But without you in my life, I discovered the only addiction I have is you. Fate brought us together. It's love that tells me we should be together."

He reached into his pocket and pulled out a small black velvet box. He opened it to reveal the most exquisite solitaire diamond ring she had ever seen. Her eyes traveled from the diamond to his eyes. He left her speechless.

"I know I lived to embrace danger. I only want to embrace you for the rest of my life. We are meant to be Lauren. I think we are incredible together. I surrender every part of me to you. Marry me?"

Lauren reached out to touch his face. She lowered herself to his level.

"I think so too. Yes, I will marry you."

He smiled.

"Happy Valentine's Day, I love you Brett."

She leaned in to meet his kiss.

He placed the ring gently on her finger as his lips met hers in a warm and tender kiss.

She smiled.

"Just so you know, I've been told I can be a little fiery at times."

"I know." He laughed.

"And I have expensive tastes," she added.

"I know that too, but you are a worthwhile lifetime investment."

He smiled slightly before his lips crushed hers in a passionate kiss.

"I love you Lauren. I always will."

I hope your Valentine's Day is hot and steamy—

and not just in the kitchen. Chocolate is known as the

elixir of love and the drink of the gods, making it perfect for Valentine's Day.

Chocolate Glazed Chocolate Tart

Falling in love is good for the heart, and so is dark chocolate.

For crust:

9 (5- by 2 1/4-inch) chocolate graham crackers (not chocolate-covered), finely ground (1 cup)

5 tablespoons unsalted butter, melted

1/4 cup sugar

For filling:

1 1/4 cups heavy cream

9 ounces bittersweet chocolate (not more than 65% cacao if marked), chopped

2 large eggs

1 teaspoon pure vanilla extract

1/4 teaspoon salt

For glaze:

2 tablespoon heavy cream

1 3/4 ounces bittersweet chocolate, finely chopped

1 teaspoon light corn syrup

1 tablespoon warm water

Equipment:

9-inch round fluted tart pan (1 inch deep)

Make crust:
Preheat oven to 350°F with rack in middle.

Stir together all ingredients and press evenly onto bottom and 3/4 inch up side of tart pan. Bake until firm, about 10 minutes. Cool on a rack 15 to 20 minutes

Make filling:
Bring cream to a boil, then pour over chocolate in a bowl and let stand 5 minutes. Gently stir until smooth. Whisk together eggs, vanilla, and salt in another bowl, then stir into melted chocolate.

Pour filling into cooled crust. Bake until filling is set about 3 inches from edge but center is still wobbly, 20 to 25 minutes. (Center will continue to set as tart cools.) Cool completely in pan on rack, about 1 hour.

Make glaze:
Bring cream to a boil and remove from heat. Stir in chocolate until smooth. Stir in corn syrup, then warm water

Pour glaze onto tart, then tilt and rotate tart so glaze coats top evenly. Let stand until glaze is set, about 1 hour.

ABOUT THE AUTHOR
ANGLEA FORD

Angela Ford originates from Nova Scotia…Canada's Ocean Playground! Her love of the ocean and sunsets are always in her heart and give her inspiration. Her love for words keeps her turning the page. She is never without a book, whether she's reading or writing. Now residing in Ontario, Angela works in Finance – numbers by day – words by night. Her dedication to volunteer and involvement with cyber safety seminars gave her an Award of Distinction and sparked the idea for her first book Closure – suspense with a dash of romance that hit the best- selling Action/Adventure. Her next release, Unforgettable Kiss, delivers a romance with a dash of suspense. Forbidden released in June 2014…Closure's sequel.

September 2014 releases Blind Tasting of The Love List series. 2014 will end with a Christmas romance The Christmas Wreath of the Forever Christmas series. Between two jobs, being a mom with a home always young adults and rather interesting stories; she is lucky to have one very patient and understanding man. But it is the furry family members who rule the house – a Puggle, two loveable cats and two unique Guinea Pigs. Every possible quiet moment she finds, she treasures and just writes about the moments to come. Angela is an avid reader of romance, a member of the RWA and Mississauga Writers Group. You can follow her at BTGN www.bookstogonow.com or visit her website/blog Romantic Escapes at http://www.angelafordauthor.com to connect with her on her social network sites. She loves to hear from her readers – they keep her smiling!

CPSIA information can be obtained at www.ICGtesting.com
Printed in the USA
LVOW04s1902020215

425350LV00037B/2249/P